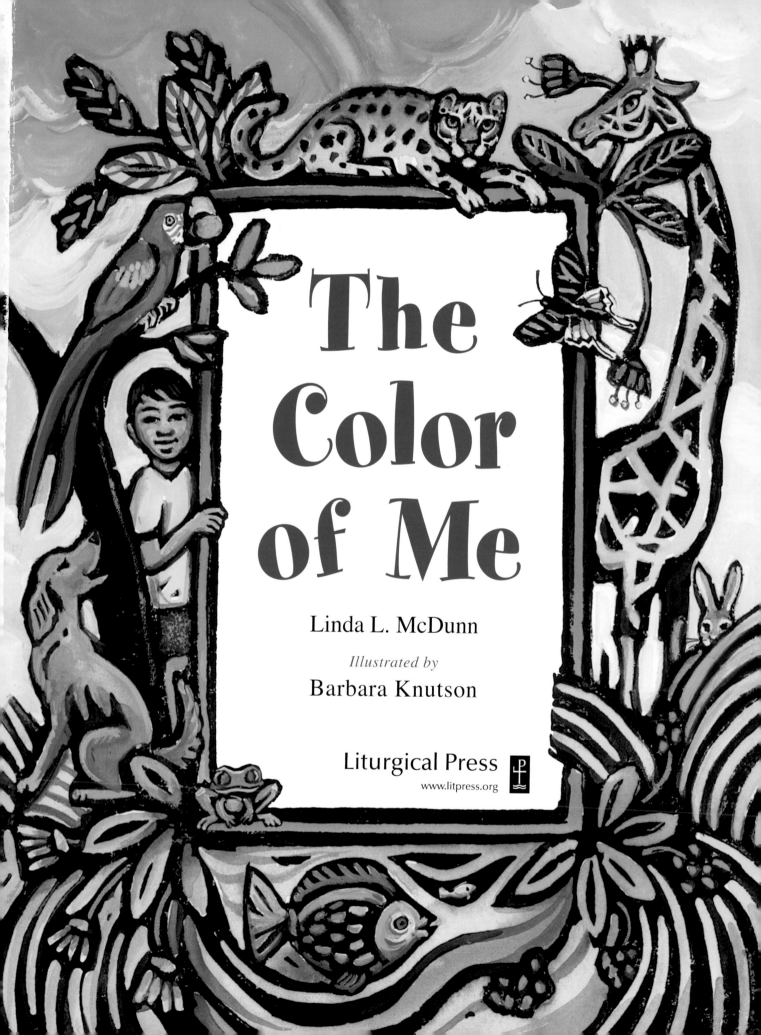

The Color of Me

Linda L. McDunn

Illustrated by

Barbara Knutson

Liturgical Press
www.litpress.org

In the very beginning of the world,
there was only darkness and nothing.

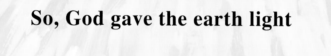

So, God gave the earth light

and saw that it was very *good* for it contained all the colors of God. Then God blessed the colors with love, life, and purpose, and with them began to create for the earth.

God created soils of color—
black soil,
red soil,
brown soil, and more,
all to give life to plants.

God saw that the soils of color were good.

God created trees of color —
with green leaves,
red leaves,
yellow leaves, and more,
all to provide shade and fruit.

God saw that the trees of color were good.

God created flowers of color —
red flowers,
purple flowers,
pink flowers, and more,
all to give beauty and fragrance.

God saw that the flowers
of color were good.

God created fish of color—
yellow fish,
blue fish,
silver fish, and more,
all to give life to the oceans.

God saw that the fish
of color were good.

God created butterflies of color—

orange butterflies,
yellow butterflies,
green butterflies, and more,
all to give beauty to the breeze.

God saw that the butterflies of color were good.

God created birds of color—
blue birds, black birds,
yellow birds, and more,
all to give song to the sky above.

God saw that the birds
of color were good.

God created rabbits of color—
white rabbits, brown rabbits,
gray rabbits, and more,
all to hop joyfully upon the land.

God saw that the rabbits of color were good.

God created dogs of color—
brown dogs, gold dogs,
black dogs, and more,
all to wag their tails with
unconditional love.

God saw that the dogs of color were good.

God created horses of color—
black horses,
white horses,
brown horses, and more,
all to race with the wind.

God saw that the horses
of color were good.

God continued to create for the earth many kinds
of soils, plants, and creatures that flew in the air,
lived on the land and in the waters.

Lastly, God created people of color—brown people,
white people, black people, red people, yellow people,
and more, all in God's own image.

God saw that the people of color were good.

God smiled and let the people know . . .

. . . that the earth and all the beautiful colors in it, the soils, the plants, the animals, and more, were given to them to live and prosper;

that special gifts were given to each person to share with one another and to care for the earth;

that people were gifts to one another, different in color but the same in heart, to take care of and to love;

and most importantly, that God would always be with them, and that the Spirit of God would speak through them. All they needed to do was quietly listen with their hearts and talk to God.

Time passed, and there came to be many people on the earth and they prospered. They cared for the earth and talked about God.

Then one day during a great gathering of people of all colors, a child questioned, "What color is God?"

For a time, there was silence.

Then one person answered,
"I believe God is blue, like the sky."

Then another
quickly said, "No,
God is brown,
like me."

Another said, "Oh, God must be
green like the plants of the earth."

Another said, "No,
God is white, like me."

Another said, "Certainly,
God is yellow, like my skin."

Another said, "God must be
orange, like the sunset."

Another said, "No, God is black, like me."

Another said, "God has to be gray, like the clouds that give forth rain."

Still another said, "No, God is red, like me."

And the people talked on and on, expressing their opinions about the color of God, until the voices became so loud that no one could hear any one person over another.

Slowly, a gentle mist of rain filled the air. Droplets fell upon the people and all the earth. The rain was so gentle, warm, and refreshing that it began to calm everyone, washing away the conflict that was building.

As the rain stopped, the child was very confused and asked the question again, "So, what color *is* God?"

At that moment a splendor of beautiful colors filled the sky. A hush came over the crowd for they were filled with wonder.

Then a person who had always quietly listened to God stepped forward and gently answered the child, "God is the same color as you." Immediately the child smiled and was very happy. Then the person continued, "And God is the same color as me, and everyone else."

Looking puzzled, the child asked, "How can that be?"

The person answered, "Because God is great and from love God created people, male and female. Each one of us is made in God's image. God is the same colors as we are. The beautiful colors in the sky are a reminder that everything and everyone is made from God's colors— the soils, the plants, the animals, and each one of us, and we are all parts of those colors, just as God is."

At that moment, the child looked up at the rainbow, then at the many different colors of people there, and exclaimed, "I like how God colored me and everyone else!"
Then, one by one, the people began to proclaim that the colors of God lived in each one of them.

From that day on, the people rejoiced in the *goodness* of God's colors, passing on the story of the rainbow to every generation, for it was known that God colors in love and that God is all colors.

For my son,
Damion,
and to those
who see the *goodness* in all colors
by listening with their hearts.

Linda L. McDunn

For my parents.   *Barbara Knutson*

Art direction and design by Ann Blattner.

Text: © 2004 by Linda L. McDunn. All rights reserved.

Illustrations: © 2004 by the Order of Saint Benedict, Collegeville, Minnesota.
All rights reserved.

Published by the Liturgical Press, Saint John's Abbey, P.O. Box 7500, Collegeville,
Minnesota 56321-7500. Printed in China.

1   2   3   4   5   6   7   8   9

McDunn, Linda L., 1951–
    The color of me / Linda L. McDunn ; illustrated by Barbara Knutson.
      p. cm.
    Summary: When people start to argue about the color of God, a beautiful rainbow
reveals that God is the colors of everyone and everything that He created.
    ISBN 0-8146-2952-0 (alk. paper)
    [1. God—Fiction. 2. Color—Fiction.]   I. Knutson, Barbara, ill.   II. Title.

PZ7.M4784465Co   2004
[E]—dc22

2004005900